Samuel French Acting Edition

Moment of Weakness

A Comedy in Two Acts

by Donald Churchill

MUSIC USE NOTE

Licensees are solely responsible for obtaining formal written permission from copyright owners to use copyrighted music in the performance of this play and are strongly cautioned to do so. If no such permission is obtained by the licensee, then the licensee must use only original music that the licensee owns and controls. Licensees are solely responsible and liable for all music clearances and shall indemnify the copyright owners of the play(s) and their licensing agent, Samuel French, against any costs, expenses, losses and liabilities arising from the use of music by licensees. Please contact the appropriate music licensing authority in your territory for the rights to any incidental music.

IMPORTANT BILLING AND CREDIT REQUIREMENTS

If you have obtained performance rights to this title, please refer to your licensing agreement for important billing and credit requirements.

Moment of Weakness was produced at the Yvonne Arnaud Theatre in Guildford with Liza Goddard, Christopher Timothy and Ruth Hudson in the starring roles. It was directed by Val May.

The play subsequently was produced at the Theatre Royal Brighton, with direction by Val May, design by Tim Shorthall and lighting Richard M. Parker.

CHARACTERS

AUDREY: Forties. Cool, elegant, delicately featured. Fairish hair. A doctor's daughter.

TONY: Late forties. Working-class upbringing. Now belongs to media class.

LUCY: Eighteen. Just started her first job on local paper. A lot of youthful vitality, but caring. Very mature for her years.

TIME: The Present.

Action of the play takes place over four days.

MOMENT OF WEAKNESS

*A cottage in Wiltshire. Early Spring. The front door centre
is open and looks out onto shrubs. There is a window to
the right of this and downstage to our right a door to a
kitchen. To the left of front door is a staircase.
Downstage left is a conservatory with green washed
windows and an overgrown vine. The furniture is
ordinary stuff from local auctions.*

A CAR is heard approaching and stopping.

*AUDREY darts from the kitchen, crouching low to avoid
being seen through the window. SHE peers through a
hole in the curtains. There is a crunch of feet on a
shingle path as someone approaches.*

*AUDREY backs, crouching, into the kitchen and bumps
into the furniture. The CAR drives off.*

TONY appears in the doorway.

TONY. Hello? (*Half enters ... knocking on open door.*)
Audrey? (*HE steps into the room, then goes out into the
conservatory. HE opens a door and calls out down the
garden.*) Ah! There you are!

AUDREY. (*Off stage. Surprised.*) Oh! You've arrived!
(*Enters through conservatory door wearing gardening
gloves and carrying a trowel and a pot of peonies in bud.
Graciously apologetic.*) So sorry! I was in the shed potting
some peonies. Been waiting long?

TONY. Just come. What are you doing to the peonies?

(*BOTH polite and reserded.*)

AUDREY. I thought I'd take a clump of them home. The Gardener's Handbook says *never* move them but the Gardening Companion says they don't mind being moved once every five years ... so perhaps they'll be okay. (*SHE puts them on a shelf.*)

TONY. You've caught them when they don't mind?

AUDREY. At exactly the right time. I've worked it out. I planted them our first summer here ten years ago.

TONY. That was eleven years ago.

AUDREY. No, no ... that was ... (*Counts on fingers.*) Oh dear. (*Looks back at peonies.*)

TONY. Perhaps peonies can't count either.

AUDREY. Well not over *ten* surely? (*Puts her gloves on the work bench in the conservatory.*) You're looking very well. (*SHE comes into the room.*)

TONY. And you. In fact I was just about to say, I haven't seen you looking as pretty for years. You look so soft and relaxed. And what have you done with your hair? Oh yes ... I know, you've stopped dyeing it. Very good. Glad you've let nature take its course.

AUDREY. (*Regarding him for a moment.*) No, I mean it, Tony. You've no paunch at all. You don't have to give me any soft soap in return. Where has that great fat belly gone? That great fat belly that used to hang over your belt as if you were smuggling a month's laundry under your shirt! I'm amazed! It's made you look years younger.

TONY. Thank you.

AUDREY. Don't misunderstand me, but may I put my arm round your waist?

TONY. Help yourself.

(SHE does so in an impersonal way and for a moment THEY stand side by side.)

AUDREY. Are you holding anything in?

TONY. No.

AUDREY. Well ... it's incredible! My hand has never reached round this far for at least seven years! Would you mind if I put both my arms round?

TONY. No.

AUDREY. *(SHE does so.)* They meet! My hands actually meet! Well! I haven't been able to do that since the miners' strike.

TONY. Have you ever wanted to do it?

AUDREY. Not very often. Well ... well ... how amazing and how irritating! All those years I nagged you about your boozing and it didn't do the slightest bit of good, then within a year of marrying someone else you're like Henry Fonda.

TONY. That is a compliment ... to be compared with him. All those years you had his photo stuck up over your sink and you never said I reminded you in the *least* of Henry Fonda. Thank you.

AUDREY. You're as slim as Henry Fonda. The resemblance stops there. Where has it gone? *(SHE opens his shirt.)* Your stomach have stretch marks like mine did after Lucy?

TONY. What do they look like?

AUDREY. I should have remembered. You never looked at any part of my body after Lucy was born. Does your stomach look slightly puckered ... like a leaky Lilo that someone has just sat on?

(HE shows his stomach.)

AUDREY. Not a sign! What did Stella say to stop you drinking?

TONY. She never mentioned it. *(Brightly.)* The old place is looking just the same. That same old scruffy look I always liked.

AUDREY. I've just spent seven hours cleaning it up!

TONY. Well I still like its scruffy look.

AUDREY. I know I'm not known for my housecraft but I promise you it was filthy! No one's been here for six months. It looked very sad when I arrived. All forgotten and abandoned ... just like the Marie Celeste.

TONY. That's a boat.

AUDREY. I'm not going to argue with you the moment I see you, Tony. I made up my mind about that. Yesterday when I was slogging away with the hoover and wiping all the paintwork ... I kept saying to myself ... when he comes tomorrow, Audrey ... you will not have a row! Please help me keep my good resolution.

TONY. I will. *(Pause, then politely.)* We were lucky not to get a burst pipe with that terrible winter we had.

AUDREY. *(Equally polite.)* Weren't we just?

(SHE smiles. HE smiles. A pause of five seconds. THEY both open their mouth to speak, but stop. Another pause, slightly shorter, then BOTH speak together.)

TONY/AUDREY. But I remember I ... Would you like ...?

TONY. So sorry.

AUDREY. No. What were you going to say?

TONY. Just that I remember now ... I tied some underfelt round the pipes in the loft in that cold winter we had five years ago.

AUDREY. That probably did the trick.

TONY. What were you going to say?

AUDREY. Just wondered if you'd like a coffee before we start?

TONY. Real coffee?

AUDREY. I do have instant.

TONY. Real instant?

AUDREY. Real instant? I do hope you're not in one of your clever dick moods today?

TONY. It's not that caffeine-less instant?

AUDREY. Just ordinary instant. But I have percolated a pot of real coffee. The sort you always adored ... high grown Columbian ... but if you prefer instant these days?

TONY. No ... no ...

AUDREY. I do, actually. In fact, I only bought the real stuff because you were coming.

TONY. Stella says it's bad for the heart.

AUDREY. She's right. How is she?

TONY. Fine. At home we drink some stuff called Schlerg.

AUDREY. Why does that ring a bell?

(The following in increasing tempo.)

TONY. It's made out of barley and German dandelions.

AUDREY. Why do you say *German* dandelions?

TONY. It's made in Germany and dandelions grow there.

AUDREY. So does barley.

TONY. But that could be imported. It travels better than dandelions. That is why I deliberately said German dandelions and not German barley.

AUDREY. I see.

(The exchange is a quick, edgy flare up, then dies.)

TONY. Thank you. Stella buys it at the health food store.

AUDREY. Do you like it?

TONY. *(Slight pause.)* It's very good for the heart.

AUDREY. You can't like it then. Nothing I like is good for me.

TONY. It's an acquired taste, like truffles.

AUDREY. I've never had a truffle.

TONY. No, nor have I.

AUDREY. What's it look like?

TONY. Like a jar of rusty iron filings with a blue label.

AUDREY. Oh yes! I remember now. Lucy bought it once.

TONY. Doesn't *smell* of dandelions at all.

AUDREY. What do dandelions smell of?

TONY. *(His voice gets a little pedantic.)* What I meant was it doesn't smell as I would have expected dandelions to smell. Not dried dandelions anyway.

AUDREY. *(Giving way.)* I see! Yes. Dried dandelions. Yes, well, I agree. It doesn't smell like anything else does it?

TONY. A strange musky smell ... like old clothes left in a damp cellar.

AUDREY. And slightly burnt.

TONY. Slightly burnt clothes?

AUDREY. No, not clothes ... burnt food. Like when you boil prunes and it boils dry and the prunes begin to catch ... that smell.

TONY. I've never boiled prunes.

AUDREY. (*Smiling.*) You've never boiled an egg in the twenty years I've known you, darling, but you can *imagine* the smell can't you?

TONY. I can *imagine* ... yes. Burnt prunes and damp clothes would come very near to the smell ... yes ... you're probably right. (*Slight pause.*) The taste *is* an acquired taste though ... you will give me that?

AUDREY. Yes.

TONY. Thank you.

AUDREY. Lucy and I never acquired it. At least she didn't up to the time she lived with me. Does she drink it with you now?

TONY. No. She has a separate jar of instant. (*Slight pause.*) It's really very nice to meet you again, Audrey.

AUDREY. (*Wary, surprised.*) What do you want?

TONY. I mean it. What's it been? Ten months?

AUDREY. Must be.

TONY. And you appear to be leading a very full life. I hear all your news from the kids. They say you and Brian seem to be working out well.

AUDREY. Yes thank you. Mark tells me you've been very busy.

TONY. Best year ever.

AUDREY. Good. You certainly look very prosperous. And *your* hair is going beautifully grey isn't it? Just like that chap in that whisky advert you did. Was it yours?

TONY. Yes. Very clever of you. I didn't know my photographic style was so distinctive.

AUDREY. It isn't. I recognised Corfe Castle in the background. I thought I bet that was Tony's idea ... shooting that butler giving that Duke a whisky as he sat in that ruined castle.

TONY. It was. They wanted a ruined castle and I remembered those holidays we had in Corfe.

AUDREY. Lovely seeing it again. Took me right back seventeen years. You're as slim now as you were then.

TONY. Thank you.

(Their warmest moment so far.)

TONY. Actually, I know exactly what Schlerg tastes like. Very weak stale coffee that's been strained through your mother's corsets.

AUDREY. Oh I am glad you said that. I was beginning to think I had maligned you all these years. In the past when people have first met you and said to me what a charming man you were, I've always told them it's simply because they've only known you five minutes. There always comes a time, I'd say, when Tony will be extremely offensive. It's such a relief to know I haven't been selling you short.

TONY. I would like a cup of high grown Columbian very much ... thank you.

(SHE exits into the kitchen. HE goes out into the conservatory. AUDREY comes out with a tray of coffee with two cups, some shortcake and a ceramic percolator.)

TONY. As you're taking the peonies, I shall take the vine.

AUDREY. Have you room in your van? It is about twenty-five feet long and the roots go next door.

TONY. It is rather big I suppose. No, I'll leave it where it is. Looks very good there.

AUDREY. Yes it does and Mrs. Trodd particularly liked it.

TONY. Mrs. Trodd?

AUDREY. The lady buying the cottage.

TONY. Ah!

AUDREY. But take it if you like. I'll ask the neighbours to dig up their fence. Please don't think I don't want you to have it.

TONY. No, it belongs here. Anyway I've only borrowed an old transit van and it'll be quite full enough by the time we've finished sorting out this junk.

AUDREY. (*Goes to the door and looks out over the front garden.*) Where is it?

TONY. Stella's driven it over to Stoke Basset to see this friend she was at school with.

AUDREY. She's come down with you?

TONY. (*Eyes her for a moment.*) Yes. I shall go over and collect it when I'm ready to load up. You won't have to meet her so don't look alarmed.

AUDREY. I was just wondering if she should be driving in her condition.

TONY. It's only a couple of miles over to Stoke. She said she wanted to.

AUDREY. You drove from London?

TONY. Of course. She said she was bored sitting at home and just waiting.

AUDREY. She must be due very soon.
TONY. In about a month.

(AUDREY pours the coffee.)

TONY. Why didn't you come out and say hello when we arrived? I do think it rather eccentric of you to go on avoiding her.
AUDREY. Funnily enough, I agree. I have been rather silly that way, but I've got over it now. I would have said hello to her had I heard you arrive, but I was in the shed at the bottom of the garden.
TONY. I don't ignore Brian, why do you ignore Stella?
AUDREY. I was in the potting shed when you arrived! I hadn't the *least* intention of ignoring your wife. I didn't even know she was coming with you, but had I *heard* or *seen* you arrive, I would most certainly have gone out, said hello and invited you both in for a cup of coffee. Well, she wouldn't like my coffee, of course, but had I been aware of your arrival, I would have been delighted to give her a cup of tea or something. I admit that in the last couple of years I haven't wanted any contact with her, but, as I say, I'm *completely* over that now. She's got her life with you, I've got mine with Brian and that's fine.
TONY. I'm glad.
AUDREY. I would have been only too delighted to invite her in for a cup of tea or something. I do know what it's like to be eight months' pregnant, Tony. I can remember that far back. Having sat in a van all the way from London she must have been dying to stretch her legs ...
TONY. She's very happy to say hello to you!

AUDREY. I'm sure.

TONY. She wants to be on good terms with you.

AUDREY. And I with her. I did go through a stage when I wanted to forget the past, but I'm over that and now I feel friendly to everyone. So ... let's sort the furniture out. Decide who takes what and then let's go our separate ways! (*SHE begins to throw book into a cardboard box.*)

TONY. That doesn't sound too friendly.

AUDREY. (*Controlled. During the following she punctuates her remarks by hurling books into various boxes.*) Darling ... I am feeling very, very friendly towards you, Stella and your dreadful mother. I haven't felt this friendly for ages! I'm *very* happy about my life and everyone in it ... past and present.

TONY. Fair enough.

AUDREY. So please—no more rows! (*Edgy, slightly strident.*) So ... let's make a start! I've got plenty of stick-on labels. (*SHE picks up a paper bag and takes them out.*) ... and three felt pens ... Black ... red and green.

TONY. (*Sips the coffee.*) Oooooh! Fantastic!

AUDREY. (*Relaxing a little.*) Oh good. Thank you. Now I thought we'd write in black those things we want to send to the auction, red for what you want and green for what I want.

TONY. Fine. Anything you say.

AUDREY. We don't *have* to do it my way. If you have an alternative suggestion let us discuss it.

TONY. What is there to discuss?

AUDREY. You've got your jaw on.

TONY. Yes, I remembered to put my jaw on.

AUDREY. That tight jaw you do when you're petulant.

TONY. Does it sometimes astonish *you* how we managed to live together without throttling each other?

AUDREY. Constantly. (*Slight pause.*) I once very nearly stabbed you with a kebab skewer. There's obviously something about my marking arrangements you don't like?

TONY. Why do you say that?

AUDREY. Because you've got your jaw on. (*Pause.*) Perhaps you'd prefer black?

TONY. I think you would prefer it. You've always been partial to a bit of black pudding haven't you?

AUDREY. I'm not looking for a fight, Tony.

TONY. Nor am I. I've just driven one hundred and thirteen miles. I'm not in a fighting mood either.

AUDREY. You know I am referring to the labels.

TONY. I do. It was one of my adolescent jokes. Any colour you like, Audrey. Black, blue with pink stripes, brown with yellow spots.

AUDREY. (*Catches sight of herself in the wall mirror and goes to it and examines her face.*) Whenever I see you, and thank God it's not often, it really upsets me how much I dislike you.

TONY. Really? I don't feel a thing. (*Slight pause.*) I suppose I should feel rather flattered you still feel something so positive. In fact, yes, I feel quite touched.

AUDREY. Oh don't be ... I'm only worried in case it shows in my face. Disliking people is so aging for a woman.

TONY. I see.

AUDREY. It gives you tramlines either side of the mouth. (*SHE goes closer.*) I've only got a suggestion of that so far.

TONY. Well I shall be gone soon and you won't have to see me again till our daughter's wedding so ...

AUDREY. I didn't know she was getting married! It's not that terrible Rodney is it? Please don't tell me that! Oh she is a devious little hussy. She never tells me anything these days! It's *not* Rodney is it, Tony? Please don't say it's Rodney! Oh God! I feel quite faint. I must sit down. (*SHE sits on the sofa beside him.*)

TONY. She's not getting married to anyone—as far as I know. I merely mentioned it because when we were chatting the other night she said that when she *did* get married she'd like us both to be there. I want my parents to dance at my wedding, she said.

AUDREY. Oh! That's all right then. It's not that he comes from ...

TONY. He comes from Bromley.

AUDREY. It's the same thing these days.

TONY. He was born in Bromley.

AUDREY. Tony! Don't split hairs. Rodney is very Turkish. Whether he was born in Bromley or Istanbul is purely a technicality ... he is a Turk! Not that I hold that against him. It's just his Turkish manner, not his complexion. It's just that I don't think Rodney is our *sort*. In the one afternoon I spent with him when Lucy brought him over for tea ... I discovered he approves of fox-hunting, hare coursing, hanging for embezzlers and public circumcision of sexual deviants. And he didn't even try the chocolate sponge cake I made specially.

TONY. He must have found it easier to talk to you. When I first met him he immediately said he believed in dowries and I went rather silent after that.

AUDREY. You gave me a terrible turn, Tony.

TONY. I'm sorry.

AUDREY. I thought I must have said the wrong thing to her the other day. I have to tread so carefully with Lucy's boyfriends.

TONY. Lucy says you walk all over them.

AUDREY. That's not true. I always treat them with the greatest courtesy. Anyway, thank God she's not marrying Rodney. It's nothing personal. It's just that I don't approve of Levantine layabouts.

TONY. Lucy calls him her Turkish Delight. Anyway, all I set out to say was that the quicker we mark up the furniture the quicker I can go and take your tramlines with me.

AUDREY. Oh yes!

TONY. So any ... arrangements you wish to make for identifying the furniture will suit me perfectly.

AUDREY. Good! (*Rises.*) So we'll mark it according to my original plan.

TONY. Great.

AUDREY. What about this easy chair? Would you like it?

TONY. Would you?

AUDREY. I'm asking you. Would it fit in with Stella's colour scheme?

TONY. What colour scheme?

AUDREY. What is the predominant colour of your living room?

TONY. Er ...

AUDREY. What style of thing has she got already? Victorian, thirties, ... very modern?

TONY. All sorts.

AUDREY. What sort of drapes? What are things mainly covered in?

TONY. Dust.

AUDREY. So this chair will fit in?

TONY. Er ...

AUDREY. What is the general feeling of the room?

TONY. That Miss Havisham lives on. But if you don't want it, I'll have it for my study. I've always liked that old chair. I bought it for ten bob in that junk shop round the corner from us in Acton.

AUDREY. I bought it actually in a second hand shop in Isleworth.

TONY. No, I bought it because it was exactly like a chair in that Renoir film "The River." I thought I was going to be another Jean Renoir then. My God! That's going back.

AUDREY. I bought it when I was seven months pregnant with Mark because I thought it would make a very comfortable nursing chair.

TONY. (*Shrugs.*) Okay.

AUDREY. It's not important.

TONY. No.

AUDREY. I'll mark it green.

TONY. By all means. You have it.

AUDREY. I'm giving it to you.

TONY. I'm red. (*A beat. SHE sighs.*) I'm not red? T't! Why is life always decisions?

AUDREY. (*Pleasant but patient.*) If you now want to be red ... you can *be* red, Tony ... Just decide what colour you want and stick to it. That's all I ask.

TONY. What am I?

AUDREY. What are you, Tony?

TONY. On second thoughts, don't tell me.
AUDREY. You're green.
TONY. Then mark it green please.

*(As SHE does so and sticks on a label TONY examines the
    plate of shortcake.)*

AUDREY. I made it specially ... as you used to love
my shortcake. But you don't have to eat it as a favour to
me.
TONY. It's got butter in hasn't it?
AUDREY. Of course.
TONY. And white sugar?
AUDREY. Yes.
TONY. And flour that has been treated with chemicals?
AUDREY. Probably.
TONY. I shall love it.
AUDREY. What's that?
TONY. (*HE takes a large bite.*) Ah well! I've just taken
forty five minutes off my life. That's what Steve says.
AUDREY. Who's he?
TONY. A friend of Stella's.
AUDREY. One of these health addicts is he?
TONY. Yes. He grows all his own stuff. Vegetables,
fruit, pot. He told me on Monday that in the month he's
been staying with us, he's seen me eat and drink twenty-
seven things which will shorten my life. I got so depressed
I had to go and have a pint of draught guinness and a
sausage roll down the pub. Anyway, he's going back to
Borth-y-Llangyderch on Friday so I've only got another
three days of watching him spray his mashed up swedes and

beetroot juice all over my dinner. Last night I had a pork chop and he said I was digging my grave with my teeth.

AUDREY. I hope you said he was totally wrong.

TONY. Is he wrong?

AUDREY. Totally.

TONY. Well that's a comfort.

AUDREY. They're not your teeth.

TONY. I've often said you should work for the Samaritans. You always know just what to say to people to give them hope for a bright tomorrow.

AUDREY. Why is this Steve staying with you?

TONY. He's come to lobby his M. P. about his Social Security money. The Welsh have cut it off.

AUDREY. Why can't he get a job?

TONY. Not sure. I think he gets too exhausted after his morning exercises. Anyway ... roll on Friday.

AUDREY. He's going back to some commune is he?

TONY. Yes, he and ten other freaks share a cow shed on this soggy hill in Wales. Stella made me spend a weekend there. It went right to my chest. I thought I was going to get my bronchial-pneumonia back again.

AUDREY. You can't afford that. It was your bronchial-pneumonia twelve years ago which made all your hair fall out.

TONY. Not at all. I distinctly remember the doctor telling me that I was losing my hair because of excessive sexual activity.

AUDREY. Who with? You made love to me once during that year you had your bronchial-pneumonia. Afterwards it was once every two years.

TONY. It worked didn't it? I've still got hair.

AUDREY. Would you like this occasional table?

TONY. Is there still woodworm in the back legs?

AUDREY. Of course. I'll mark it for auction. (*SHE writes out a label.*) ... in black. (*Slight pause.*) I don't suppose you will ever stop laughing at me about Jamaica. We meet so rarely these days but you still can't resist getting in a quick dig can you?

TONY. I never quite know where I am with your racial prejudice. I've obviously said something which has offended your Jamaican partiality. What? (*Frowns.*) Let me try and recollect. (*Slight pause.*) Those Watergate tapes were such a good idea weren't they? If we had installed recorders in our living room and bedroom, it would have saved us such a lot of rows.

AUDREY. It would have been no good putting one in our bedroom. You never talked to me in our bedroom in the twenty years of our marriage. All you'd get on the tape is eight hours of snoring with the odd trumpeting fart as light relief.

TONY. I see you've been reading Barbara Cartland again. (*Slight pause.*) Ah yes! I've got it! I intended my remark about black pudding to come under the heading of good humoured banter. I didn't mean it offensively. If you were upset by the remark I apologise unreservedly. We've got an entire house of furniture to sort out and I just made one of my little quips to jolly us along. If you consider my remark in bad taste—forgive me. Elroy, who is currently my focus man, comes from Barbados and is as black as your hat. We worked on a salami commercial last week and we never stopped making jokes about black pudding and liver sausage. We don't pretend our skins are the same colour. We just laugh about our differences. We find them a rich source for further school-boy humour.

AUDREY. I'm sure. As our trip to Jamaica has proved to be. For seven years now you've been ridiculing me about it.

TONY. I ...

AUDREY. But did you ever realise that when we went there I was a woman whose morale, self confidence and pride had been totally destroyed?

TONY. I don't remember it occurring to me ... no ... but why go into ...?

AUDREY. (*Furious.*) Because you're still making fun of me two years after we're divorced! I owe you nothing, Tony. I never did you a bad turn in Jamaica in fact, the reverse! You've no right to keep ridiculing me about what happened. I don't keep dredging up the things you did—and my God, I could! And I only know about two of the women you had during that time we lived in Putney, and that's only because they were both my best friends. But I don't mention it. You are no longer married to me, so the few times we meet I try and treat you with the same respect and courtesy I treat everyone else ... you bastard.

TONY. Do you want this sofa?

AUDREY. No!

TONY. Nor do I!

AUDREY. No! It's time I told you exactly what you owe to George. The man you've derided for years!

TONY. I don't see how either of us can ...

AUDREY. When you reluctantly agreed to take me with you to Jamaica I had given up trying to make myself desirable to you. There was no point. I knew I was no longer attractive because you had rejected me so many times. I didn't try to make myself attractive to George ... or to any man because I was convinced I'd just suffer further humiliation. When George made love to me I just could not believe it was happening. Not to me! That is how low I was when you took me to Jamaica.

TONY. Are you saying that George did, in fact, give you one?

AUDREY. Oh come off it, Tony. You've always known, but *not* what it meant to me. You knew that day we came back to the hotel after a tour of George's farm.

TONY. After that tour of the mango plantation?

AUDREY. Yes. You knew. So don't be ridiculous. Don't start pretending you never knew. Not now. Not after all these years ... please. Don't insult my intelligence.

TONY. I never knew—and I remember that day well. When you arrived back at the hotel that evening ... the unit had had a very hard day's shooting and I remember being very tired and all I wanted to do was sit outside in the shade and have one of those cold pineapple drinks you suck with a straw. Perhaps I wasn't at my most alert but I promise you ... as far as I knew you had just come back from a tour of the mango plantation.

AUDREY. You knew Tony. (*Sighs.*) Please ... don't let's have any of these ridiculous charades of yours. This refusal to face reality. This stupid pretence of ignorance. You always knew that George had made love to me on a pile of mangoes ...

TONY. Pardon? I'll have to have another piece of shortcake. Must keep my strength up for this.

AUDREY. And the mangoes stained my frock because they were very ripe. That is why I had to buy a new dress before I got back to the hotel. That is how you knew.

TONY. What was it like?

AUDREY. Cream with pink polka dots.

TONY. No, being had on a pile of mushy mangoes?

AUDREY. I wouldn't dream of pandering to your perverted sexual fantasies by describing the scene.

TONY. Right. Forget it.

(Pause.)

AUDREY. But I will say, in passing, that ... it was absolutely divine!

TONY. I can imagine.

AUDREY. Anyway ... that is how you knew.

TONY. How? I've lost the thread. It's like when we used to go and see those early French films without sub-titles and you used to translate for me, but it always took you ten minutes to work it out. I remember we saw that thriller once and it wasn't till we were going home in the bus did I find out who'd done it.

AUDREY. You knew I had been unfaithful to you the moment I got back to the hotel. You were sitting out in front under one of those umbrellas and you knew at once that the dress I was wearing was not the dress I wore when I went out with him in the morning.

TONY. Well I suppose I might have put two and two together ... or one and one together and a lot of squashy mangoes ... but I didn't. Was I likely to remember what dress you wore when you drove off in the morning in that horse and cart?

AUDREY. You knew, Tony. It was white with blue cornflowers.

TONY. You never, never told me about having it off on a pile of mangoes.

AUDREY. There was no need. I took one look at your face and knew that you knew. That was why I never denied it.

TONY. You never denied it because I never asked you!

AUDREY. You're irritating me now, Tony. You have known for seven years I had an affair with George in Jamaica. So please don't play games!

TONY. An affair! You mean you went back to the mangoes for seconds?

AUDREY. No ... we went up to our room in the hotel.

TONY. You got a *room* with George?

AUDREY. You know perfectly well what I mean, Tony. Our room!

TONY. Our room!?

AUDREY. Yes.

TONY. With the balcony looking over the sun drenched Caribbean?

AUDREY. We didn't do it looking over the Caribbean. We were very discreet. And he was an absolute Godsend ... the things he did for my morale. It was he and he alone who made it possible for me to live with you when we got back to Putney. The thought of George has been a wonderful solace to me over the years. Thinking of him helped me keep the family together till the children had grown up.

TONY. I swear to you I never knew.

AUDREY. (*Hesitates.*) Then why have you ridiculed me about George for so long?

TONY. Because you always reacted in such a rewarding way whenever I mentioned Jamaica and George. You always went off like a penny whistle and that was fun, just innocent fun, for a sadist like me. But I never believed ...

Well, yes, he might have held your hand—but it never occurred to me you had actually *done* something!

AUDREY. Because the thought that some other man might find me attractive was inconceivable to you?

TONY. I dunno. I can't think. I'm so astonished that all these years have passed and you never told me.

AUDREY. You knew, Tony. You damn well knew! Later that evening you caught me washing the dress and asked me how I got mango stains all down the back.

TONY. What did you say?

AUDREY. I said I sat on one.

TONY. Well I'd have believed that. Sounds very likely. There's a lot of mangoes in Jamaica. I might have queried it if you had sat on a mango in Putney. Seven years ago that is. There's a lot of mangoes in Putney now, of course.

AUDREY. You don't believe me do you? You're still laughing! You can't face the fact that the one time I was physically unfaithful to you was with a black man?

TONY. If you say so.

AUDREY. You think this is just some spiteful invention of mine, made up in order to hurt you?

TONY. I don't know what I feel. I know I'd rather not discuss it.

AUDREY. (*Her emotion now painful, revealing.*) But you'd rather not discuss anything! You've always insisted that our marriage be conducted on the level of jokey chat. One must never go too deep into anything. Our relationship always had to remain on the surface ... skittering along like one of those stones you used to throw that bounced along the water. (*Slight pause.*) Okay. Perhaps it *is* a bit late in the day to mention it, but you ridiculed me once too often, Tony. (*SHE searches her bag, then exits into the kitchen. Returns with a tissue and goes to the window.*)

TONY. I'm sorry.

AUDREY. (*Softly.*) That's all right. Just don't go on pretending you didn't know.

TONY. I will now swear to you the most solemn, sacred oath a free-lance cameraman can ever make. I swear to you ... if I never work again ... I swear to you I never knew you were had seven years ago by George on a pile of Jamaican mangoes.

AUDREY. (*Pause. SHE has now recovered and is hard again.*) Well ... you're even thicker than I thought. Your mind has *completely* gone. That's all I can say. You never had much of a memory but since you've been living with Stella ... It's obviously gone completely ... (*Almost as if she is chatting brightly to herself.*) When you left me for a younger woman I fully expected you to have a heart attack. It happens all the time to these middle-aged men who suddenly leave their middle-aged wives and marry some young girl. I know two who have died inside five years. Coronary ... heart attack ... the excitement is all too much for them. I expected your heart attack but I didn't expect the mental decay! That's why I was so surprised to see you looking so fit. I thought ... My God he looks good. I didn't realise your mind had gone! And I'm pleased. It shows there's some justice left ... Talking to you nowadays is just like talking to Uncle Stanley. He went out into his garden the other day and forgot to put on his trousers ... It wouldn't have been so bad if he hadn't decided to climb up his pear tree and prune the top branches. The whole village came to look. I do see though it must be a terrible strain having to keep up with a woman twenty

years younger than you. Especially as she's also stopped
you boozing. And I don't blame her in the least. No young
woman could fancy that great paunch of yours pounding up
and down on top of her ... Well I hand it to her, she's
succeeded where I failed ... But the strain of having to keep
on your toes must affect you somewhere. If not physically,
then mentally. I do see that. Your brain has gone addled.
     TONY. FOR CHRIST'S SAKE! *(Pause.)*

(Silence.)

     AUDREY. It was only a week in Jamaica, with me
tagging along as the dreary wife of the trendy cameraman,
but it was the only week in my life when I felt a fulfilled
woman.
     TONY. Our two children have given you no fulfillment
at all, of course?
     AUDREY. They have made me a mother and as such
given me maternal fulfillment ... yes ... certainly. I love
them. I feel very grateful to have had them and very
gratified that they've grown up to be caring adults.

(Pause.)

     TONY. Well I'm pleased to hear that you have *one*
happy memory of our time together.
     AUDREY. Would *you* like this sofa?
     TONY. No, thank you. We don't have the room.
     AUDREY. I'll mark it for the sale room. (*SHE does
so.*)

(Another fast skirmish.)

TONY. You must have room. Brian has got this big house in Reigate.

AUDREY. So?

TONY. Well he must have room.

AUDREY. Why would I want him to have my sofa?

TONY. I don't know.

AUDREY. You must think I am shortly going to live with him...?

TONY. I thought you might ...

AUDREY. Who told you?

TONY. No one ...

AUDREY. It was Lucy wasn't it? She's told you everything I told her in the strictest confidence.

TONY. No ... no ... not at all.

AUDREY. (*Furious.*) She swore to me she'd never tell you. I really am very cross with her. She wormed it all out of me just because she wanted to tell *you*. I really am very cross Tony!

TONY. I promise you ... I know nothing about you and Brian.

AUDREY. She told you that I couldn't make up my mind about Brian?

TONY. No. Can't you make up your mind?

(*Pause.*)

AUDREY. It's none of your business.

TONY. I agree.

AUDREY. And whether I move in with him with my furniture is completely in the melting pot and totally my own affair.

TONY. It is.

AUDREY. What else did she tell you?

TONY. Nothing.

AUDREY. Did she tell you ...?

TONY. What?

AUDREY. I don't wish to discuss it. I don't want that sofa.

TONY. I'd have it like a shot if we had room.

AUDREY. I've got a sofa already.

TONY. That old brown one? Why don't you get rid of that and take this? We always said this sofa was better than the one we had in London didn't we?

AUDREY. We did, but I don't want it. It will remind me of something I want to forget.

TONY. What?

AUDREY. I forget. You've got me so upset telling me about Lucy telling you things I told her confidentially, it's gone completely out of my head. But it will come back. There *is* something very nasty about that sofa and it will come back to me. I *know* it's got unhappy memories for me.

TONY. But you can't remember what they are?

AUDREY. It's something to do with you.

TONY. All your unhappy memories are.

AUDREY. Either you said something dreadful on it or you did something dreadful on it.

TONY. But the sofa is not to blame.

AUDREY. I don't want it in my home.

TONY. With Brian?

AUDREY. That is not decided yet.

TONY. Why not?

AUDREY. You are a rotten swine. You know exactly why not. Lucy has told you everything. Admit it. She'll never know you told me. Promise. I know she only told you because she thought you might be able to help me. She's very wise. She knows that if you're in the mood you can be very good at sorting people out. That would be her motive in telling you and I can forgive her for that.

TONY. She did say to me that you couldn't make up your mind about Brian. He wants to marry you but you'd like to live with him a bit first.

AUDREY. True.

TONY. But his eighty-four year old aunt lives at the back of his house.

AUDREY. Eighty-five.

TONY. And though *he* wouldn't mind you coming to live with him in sin in Reigate, she does.

AUDREY. Right.

TONY. She would be delighted to have you living there as Brian's wife ...? but not as his mistress.

AUDREY. Spot on.

TONY. So you suggested putting her into a home.

AUDREY. A nice home for retired gentlefolk.

TONY. And Brian said that'll kill her within three months. Not kill her immediately. She'll just have enough time to change her will leaving her money to her other nephew in America who has always been her favourite till Brian offered her the flat at the back of his house?

AUDREY. Yes.

TONY. But money aside ...

AUDREY. Yes ... money aside ...

TONY. He is, in fact, very fond of his Aunty Ruth and doesn't want to upset her last few years.

AUDREY. He does love his Aunty Ruth.

TONY. And he loves you too?

AUDREY. In his funny way.

TONY. And he's desperate to get married to anyone?

AUDREY. Not anyone, but he does say that since Brenda walked out and took the kids, he's only felt half a person.

TONY. Which half? No, I didn't mean that. I could cut my tongue out. Well now, up to about a month ago you were quite happy to jog along and not do anything.

AUDREY. Yes.

TONY. But a new complication has arisen in the form of Hilary.

AUDREY. Helen.

TONY. A woman he loved when he was twenty-one but she married someone else and went to live in Australia, and has now come back as a rich attractive widow ...

AUDREY. She's not in that good nick. She's got to be size 16.

TONY. But she has one trump card you don't have ... she is mad keen to marry Brian and live in Reigate and look after his aunt.

AUDREY. She's actually proposed to him.

TONY. Well they do it differently down under. Brian is immensely flattered, of course, and finds it very appealing to be proposed to by the woman who turned him down twenty-five years ago. And the fact that she now owns a thirty thousand acre vineyard producing excellent white wine north of Sydney ... does not lessen her appeal.

AUDREY. Right.

TONY. But it also appeals to her Australian neighbour called Bruce oddly enough. A widower who has twenty thousand acres of *red* wine because with her thirty thousand acres of white wine coupled with his twenty thousand of red they could make a lot of rosé.

AUDREY. Right.

TONY. But she has a softer spot for Brian than she does have for Bruce.

AUDREY. Yes.

TONY. But she's not that soft. She's said if he doesn't accept her proposal by Friday the 13th ...

AUDREY. That's right. This Friday.

TONY. She's going back to Australia and have a marriage of true vines.

AUDREY. And I didn't think Lucy was listening to a word I said.

TONY. There you are.

AUDREY. Just wait till I see the little bitch.

TONY. Now Audrey ... You promised! If you tell her ... she'll never tell me another thing about your love life and I'd find that a sad loss ... because it *does* fascinate me.

AUDREY. Yet for some reason she hasn't told you about the one thing that still stops me saying yes?

TONY. Of course she has. That was her entire purpose in telling me the saga. She wanted to know if I could suggest some way of resolving it for you.

AUDREY. I really am very fond of Brian. He's very kind, considerate ... loving ... all the things you're not. But he is tidy.

TONY. And when you've gone to bed you can't stand him coming into the room and picking your knickers up?

AUDREY. She needn't have been that explicit. He never criticises me for my untidiness. He never says a word ... it's just that as I lie there and watch him go round picking up my things ... it drives me raving ... well ... I do find a certain difficulty in adjusting to it. Very silly of me because not once has he ever criticised me ... not once ... for anything ... I've tried to match his tidiness. I've really tried to be very tidy. Every time he comes over for supper I'm up at dawn with my hoover and brillo pads ... but then he arrives and does it all over again. And much better than me! But it's picking my things up just before he comes to bed ... That's what I find difficult ... well not difficult ... just slightly uncomfortable to live with. (*Pause.*) Well? *Have* you any helpful suggestion?

TONY. Yes. Go to bed after him. Then you won't have to lie in bed watching him go round the room picking up your underwear.

AUDREY. He's very sweet and kind to me in *every* way ... it's just that he does like things shipshape.

TONY. You'll adjust if you want to. You adjusted to my habits.

AUDREY. Ah *yes*! I know what I don't like about this sofa!

TONY. What?

AUDREY. No—it's gone again.

AUDREY. What about this corner cupboard?

TONY. You have it.

AUDREY. Right. (*SHE writes out a label.*)

TONY. Yes ... your way is much the best. We've never been able to talk. We've never been straight with each other, why try now?

AUDREY. Exactly.

TONY. I wish you hadn't lied to me when I arrived though. Such a silly lie. So unnecessary. I know you saw us arrive. You could so easily have come out and for once

... just for once ... said hello to Stella ... how's it going? But no ... you couldn't. Not even once. You couldn't just make one kind gesture towards her. She was dying to go to the loo actually. That would be ridiculous ... but you knew that today is probably the last time your paths will cross ... You could have come out and been polite to her ... if only for a few moments. But no ... you couldn't...

(Pause.)

AUDREY. I wasn't sure if you'd bring her. You didn't say you would on the phone last week but I had a feeling you wouldn't come alone. Then this morning I thought no, ... she's eight months pregnant ... she's not going to want to come all this way. Then I remembered she had this friend in Stoke. She's coming I thought, so I rushed round and tidied everything up. I made up my mind that today ... I was going to see her and invite her in and be as nice and kind as I possibly could. All morning I kept rushing to the window ... Then suddenly I heard the car. I looked out and saw you help her out of the van ... and she looked so beautiful ... so radiantly happy about having her first baby ... and I couldn't move. I watched you both look at the cottage and then talk to each other ... then you helped her into the driving seat ... and you waved ... and she smiled, looking so lovely, her life in front of her and you smiled back and suddenly I just couldn't move. I meant to. I meant to go out and be charming and generous, forgiving and mature—all the things a woman of my age should be in my circumstances, but somehow my legs wouldn't move. All my resentment, my anger suddenly welled up and rooted me to the spot.

TONY. I didn't expect you to clasp her to your bosom ... just a few pleasant words would have done.

AUDREY. It wasn't the sight of her that made me cross, it was you. But I wasn't even cross with you, just with life. Life suddenly made me very cross. It seemed so unfair. You see ...? About three or four years ago it began to dawn on me that I had had the best bit of my life in terms of having my children and seeing them grow up then leave home ... but I always knew that you and I would stay together. Live out the fag end of it together ... consoling each other about growing old ... sharing the realisation that the petrol in our tanks wouldn't last for ever though we still had enough for a lot of fun ... but ... that's not how it's turned out. That's why I couldn't go out and be nice because I saw you standing there waving goodbye to your young, expectant wife because I realised you had started all over again and I can't. All I can expect now is rheumatism, a hysterectomy and increasing difficulty reading the A to Z street guide.

(A CAR is heard approaching and stopping.)

AUDREY. That'll be Mr. Culshaw from the sale rooms come to see what we want him to take. I thought we'd be finished by now.

TONY. We haven't got far.

AUDREY. I'll tell him I'll phone him.

TONY. *(Looks out of the window.)* Oh! It's Stella.

(AUDREY goes to the window and looks out. SHE seems annoyed. SHE moves away and occupies herself.)

TONY. (*Returns and runs around the room in blind panic.*) We've got to get to London. She says her water has broken. The baby is coming—we should make London in three hours.

AUDREY. She can't possibly go back to London.

TONY. Well, what do we do? What's best? Get an ambulance?

AUDREY. No ... take her immediately to Salisbury General ... lie her down in the back of the van with her feet up ... I'll come and help you.

TONY. Oh God ... My knees have gone. I'm not made for this!

AUDREY. Come on, there should be plenty of time to get her to Salisbury. Nothing to worry about, Tony.

(THEY exit.
A CAR DOOR slams. Pause. AUDREY comes back in. Looks up a number. The CAR starts and drives off. SHE dials.)

AUDREY. Emergency maternity please. Oh hello? Maternity Sister please. Well could I speak to Sister Papadopolous then please? Oh hello Sister, there's a woman on her way to you who is about to give birth. Well she was down here from London and I think the journey has suddenly triggered it off. Her name is Mrs. Holland. She should be with you in about fifteen minutes. Contractions every twenty minutes but the water has broken. No ... I'm not exactly a friend ... more a sort of ... relative ... I'm Mrs. Holland. That's right ... the other lady is too ... She's my husband's wife you see ... (*Crossly.*)

Yes ... of course I mean second ... He's not one of those. His father was rural dean of Chipping Norton.

(LIGHTS fade ...
LIGHTS up.
Early evening.
A CAR arrives.
AUDREY comes down the stairs carrying a small over-
    night bag.
TONY appears at the open door.
SHE stops and regards him.)

TONY. A girl.
AUDREY. Congratulations.
TONY. Thank you. Seven pounds four ounces.
AUDREY. Lovely! (*Her attitude is brisk, bright and* decisive.)
TONY. And Stella's fine. No problems. The doctor said it was very straightforward. Just like shelling peas he said.
AUDREY. I'm sure. She's so young and healthy. (*AUDREY goes into the kitchen and comes out with a plastic bucket containing a bottle of champagne hidden within.*) I bought a bottle of champagne to wet the baby's head. I'm sorry it's not a proper ice bucket.
TONY. How very kind. (*HE begins to open the bottle.*)
AUDREY. You have to wet the baby's head. Will Stella mind you having a glass of champagne?
TONY. She never once told me to stop drinking, Audrey. It was a decision I came to entirely on my own.
AUDREY. I'm glad.
TONY. The Sister said you phoned. Well she was a bit confused. She said Stella's mother-in-law had called.

(HE opens the champagne.
AUDREY holds out two glasses and he pours it out.)

AUDREY. Well ... here's to Juliet.

TONY. Yes ... here's to her. (*HE sips his drink.*) God ... this champagne is marvellous. I can see why I devoted most of my life to booze.

AUDREY. As Stella won't have any of her things with her, I've put a couple of my nighties and some talcum powder in this bag with a hair brush and some hand lotion. Just a few oddments she might find handy. And take her handbag. You do need a bit of lipstick after the trauma of having a baby. So how does it feel to be a proud father for the third time?

TONY. I don't know.

AUDREY. I'm very pleased, Tony. Now that it's actually happened and you've got your brand new daughter with your brand new wife, I really am very pleased for you.

TONY. I ...

AUDREY. I do mean that. Oh, in the last year I kept on wishing it was happening to me, but suddenly ... I don't any more. Not now ... now it's actually happened. After all I've had my time. Had my babies. I've had a good part of your life and as Stella said to me that memorable day she knocked on my front door, and said "You've had him long enough ... it's my turn now!" ... well she's right. It is her turn now! (*SHE goes to him and kisses him.*) Be happy, Tony. That's all I can say to you now.

TONY. Thank you. I think I might get pissed.

AUDREY. Well proud fathers do, don't they?

TONY. I've been thinking ... what you said to me about George.

AUDREY. No. That's finished, I was very silly. It's just that you suddenly made me rather cross and because I was upset I wanted to upset you. It was very silly and petty of me. And what does it matter? It was years ago and I'd no right to rake it all up. I'm sorry.

TONY. Is it true?

AUDREY. What does it matter whether it's true or not? Both of us have got new lives to lead now. Neither of us are going to win anything fighting our old battles over again.

TONY. I agree. It's totally irrelevant now to both of us. (*Pause.*) Is it true though?

AUDREY. Yes, but totally irrelevant to the present and that's what we've both got to think of isn't it? You with Stella and Juliet and me with my new life with Brian.

TONY. Oh! So you've decided. (*Pause.*) Audrey ... tell me... why did we get divorced?

AUDREY. Very simple. You found someone who didn't have my deficiencies as a wife. Someone who gave new life to your sex drive which I had bored into atrophy. Someone twenty years younger who shored up your vanity. Someone who every time she looked in a mirror didn't say to herself ... My God! I never meant to get this old! Someone who didn't always forget to buy your favourite bacon. Someone who didn't make their own dresses and didn't have bits of them spread all over the house for six months. Who didn't have half a skirt on the sofa with a needle sticking out which you sat on ... Who didn't put cups of coffee on your scripts and make a brown ring ...

someone who didn't go to bed in a summer dress because their nightie was dirty ...

TONY. Shall *I* tell you why we foundered?

AUDREY. No thank you.

TONY. Three years ago when I left you to go and live on my own in my one room I never thought it would lead to a divorce. I didn't think about our marriage at all in fact. All I knew was that I was the highest paid cameraman working in commercials, drinking four bottles of claret a day and I was very unhappy. I didn't know how to change my life but I knew I had to. My liver was already grossly enlarged and terminal cirrhosis seemed just a crate of St. Emilion away.

AUDREY. You just walked out on me. No discussion. Just a note saying you'd gone to sort yourself out and you'd be in touch. We'd been married all those years and you were in some kind of crisis and you couldn't even discuss it with me.

TONY. Because only I had the answers ... locked somewhere inside my seventeen stone frame. For a month I did nothing.

AUDREY. You did send me a card now and then saying you were alive, but no address.

TONY. ... then I realised I must go back in my life to a time when I didn't just think about money or booze ... just work. I went back and back to when I was nineteen ... and stopped there. My first year as an art student, when I'd never heard of pack shots, zoom lenses or J. Walter Thomson. ... I went out and bought some stuff and I began to paint. Morning, noon and night I painted. I realised that that is what I had always wanted to do. After about my 73rd painting I came face to face with my trouble. That I

was a first class cameraman but could not enjoy my
success because I could not forget I was a third class
painter. I phoned you the same day I knew I'd sorted myself
out. I never thought of a divorce. But when you came over
and looked at my work and said had I passed up the chance
of earning thousands just for this? ... I knew we were
finished. You were uninvolved with my disappointment.
You laughed and didn't want to know. That is why we got
divorced.

AUDREY. According to the book of Tony.

TONY. Because you didn't want to know enough about
me. You were happy with the external. Telling me to stop
boozing because you were ashamed of my fat stomach.
You never once asked why I drank. Why should it occur to
you that I was a disappointed man? In your eyes, I was a
success. A highly paid cameraman. You only ever worked
on what you could see. For years I used to say ... I've got
to stop. Take a year off. Do nothing. Just stare. You
always said, don't be ridiculous. How can you be unhappy
with the money you make? But I was and you never
believed me, never wanted to know.

AUDREY. When we got married you were a stills
photographer for that news agency. You said you had tried
to survive as a painter for three years but realised you'd
never make it and that your true talent was as a
photographer. In the years that followed you might have
said twice you would have liked to be a painter. I remember
once I bought you a whole set of oil paints for your
birthday. But you never used them. They just went upstairs
and stayed there gathering dust. You left me because you
were bored with me dear! Bored! So please none of this
Gauguin crap about going off to your one room in

Hackney and discovering yourself. We all know that as a painter you have nothing to say but that as a documentary photographer your work has touched and maybe enlightened thousands of lives. That one you did on the Vietnam children ... that one on the slums in Mexico ... but then you sold out to the glossies and the next time you went there it was for an anti-perspirant ad ... with a glamorous model in a prettily ragged dress climbing the steps of an Aztec temple ... so that she could reach the top and squirt herself with the latest roller ball easy glide on heavenly fragrant deodorant with built in man appeal. And you *loved it!* You loved your latest BMW. It was you who wanted a kidney shaped swimming pool in our garden in Putney. You were born to do documentaries. That thing you did on the vagrants. It had a compassion that wasn't cloying, a humour that wasn't patronising and even now I cry, when I think about the one you did on that ex-Major who couldn't get a job and you followed him around watching him fill in his days with time killing, pain killing trivialities. Fourteen years ago you arrived at what you were meant to do in this life, but a packet of Birds Eye Fish Fingers came along and knocked you silly. You're a chocolate box painter but a masterly recorder of human distress—but are you going to listen to me now? Even when I was your wife I couldn't stop you wanking your talent away.

(A PHONE rings. AUDREY picks it up.)

AUDREY. Hello! Hello darling! Hold on. (*To Tony.*) It's Brian.

TONY. Ah! The door mat. I'll be off. Speak to you later.

AUDREY. Oh darling ... how lovely to hear you ! I'm so pleased you could call back. Oh no ... that was fine. I wanted to tell you. I didn't want to wait till tomorrow. I wanted to tell you my answer today. Yes please, I would like to marry you. (*Pause*.) If you still want me that is. What a relief! You sure you haven't had second thoughts? No. (*Pause*.) Yes. And I loved it. If you hadn't given me your ultimatum I'd have gone on ... shilly-shallying, as you say, for years. And I love you, darling ... thank you for bringing me so nicely to the boil. (*Briskly*.) I'd like to be married this week. Have you got something better to do this Thursday? That's the earliest day we can get married by Special Licence. I went into the Salisbury Marriage Registry this afternoon and found out all about it. Do you mind a Registry Office wedding? I'm sorry. I don't mean to be bossy. I don't *mean* to be ... I mean as we're both divorced and both had church weddings we can't get married in a church again. Three-fifteen. I've made a provisional booking. In Salisbury. I thought it would be nice to get done locally. We've got our two witnesses. Jack and Bob. Two car park attendants next to the Registry Office. They're old age pensioners and the Registrar often uses them. They charge ten pounds each and are very pleased to earn a bit of pin money. Yes ... they're standing by to close the car park at three ten next Thursday. I've had a wonderful day, Brian. A wonderful day of decision! (*SHE starts to cry*.) It's all right, Brian. I'm only crying because I'm so happy!

CURTAIN

ACT II

Three days later.

Several items of furniture are labelled in green. TONY comes down the stairs carrying sections of a baby's cot and a mattress wrapped in newspapers. HE stands it up and goes into the kitchen and returns with a brush. HE brushes off the dust then removes the old newspaper. The mattress is stained. HE picks up a piece of the newspaper and glances at an old headline.

TONY. (*Reads.*) M.P. resigns over sex scandal. Nothing changes does it? My goodness! (*He screws it up. HE stands the end of the cot against the sofa and hooks on the base-part, then hooks other end onto foot part of cot. HE stands back. The base slopes.*) No ... that can't be right. (*HE reverses the end and hooks it up. It is level. HE puts one of the wooden sides up to the side of the cot and pushes a rod through the top screw eye, into the top and bottom holes of the panel, then into lower screw eye so that the side is now hinged. HE opens it like a door.*) Right. Now we're getting somewhere. (*HE gets the other panel and hangs it on the other side, then places the mattress inside on the wire base.*) Perfect. (*HE closes the hinged side briskly and the other side falls off. HE regards it for a moment then goes round and picks it up. As HE holds it up again the cot keels over to the floor. HE stares at it then hears a car arrive. HE opens the front door and looks out for a moment then calls.*) So glad you're here! I'm having trouble with our old cot.

AUDREY. (*Enters carrying some parcels.*) So glad *you're* here! I'm having trouble with my shopping. Will you bring it in for me?

(*TONY goes out. AUDREY looks at the cot then takes out a dress from her dress bag and hangs it up. TONY returns with a cardboard box of groceries.*)

AUDREY. Thank you.

(*HE puts it down on the table.*)

AUDREY. Stella got my note then?

TONY. Yes. With the flowers. She was very touched.

AUDREY. (*Crisply.*) How nice. She's well?

TONY. Full of beans. You'd never think she had a baby four days ago.

AUDREY. I knew it would be easy for her. She has those wonderful peasant hips. And little Juliet?

TONY. (*Tersely.*) Coming along nicely. Thank you. (*Then immediately, not wishing further discussion.*) It's all right me taking these items? (*HE indicates the marked furniture.*)

AUDREY. Of course. As I said in my note take what you want. (*SHE takes out a little hat from a bag and tries it on.*)

TONY. Yes ... well just these bits... if you don't want them?

AUDREY. Not at all.

TONY. Thank you.

AUDREY. I'm glad that's all settled. I knew it would be if I let you alone. When we're together we get each other so aereated!

TONY. We do ... (*HE frowns at the cot.*)

AUDREY. But I was very glad to have seen you on Monday.

TONY. And me ...

AUDREY. It suddenly made things very clear!

TONY. Yes ... it clarified a lot of things for me too ...

AUDREY. Oh I am pleased! I'm glad you got something out of it too! You don't think this hat is a bit coy?

TONY. No. It's very nice. Are you going to Ascot or something?

AUDREY. No. I hate horses. You know that!

TONY. (*Slight pause. HE goes back to studying the cot.*) What did it clarify for you?

AUDREY. It suddenly jolted me into reality. Made me realise I was just idling my life away. When you left I suddenly felt very decisive about things.

TONY. What?

AUDREY. Well Brian for instance. I realised very clearly that he and I couldn't go on wittering like this so I told him straight. I just couldn't continue the same relationship with him.

TONY. You may think this is a funny thing for me to say but I'm pleased. Did he take it well?

AUDREY. What?

TONY. Well when you spoke to him ... when you gave him the elbow?

AUDREY. The elbow? I'm marrying him at three fifteen this afternoon!

TONY. Ah! (*HE nods then smiles, hard.*) I'm pleased about that too!

AUDREY. I knew you would be. You can stop my alimony now.

TONY. True. But that wasn't the *first* thought that came into my head!

AUDREY. What was?

TONY. I thought ... (*HE regards her like a man who has had an emotional slap in the face.*) ... what a nice day you've got for it.

AUDREY. (*Brightly.*) Yes aren't I lucky? We're coming back here after the ceremony and Lucy is going to propose a little toast to us. That'll be nice won't it?

TONY. Very nice. When is she arriving?

AUDREY. On the ten-ten. She's not coming to the Registry Office. I didn't fancy my daughter watching me get married somehow. She wanted to, of course. In fact she wanted to give me away.

TONY. (*Hardening.*) Well she would. You know Lucy ... anything for a laugh.

(*SHE gives him a cool look.*)

TONY. So that's why you've got the hat?

AUDREY. Do you like my outfit? (*SHE takes it and holds it up against herself.*) Not too dressy is it?

TONY. Just right. (*HE is getting tighter lipped but determined to smile.*)

AUDREY. Oh I am glad. You've got many faults, Tony ... but you do have very good taste. (*SHE puts it over a chair.*) I'd better organise this food. I won't have time later because we're catching the six o'clock ferry to

Jersey. Just a little honeymoon, for a couple of days. (*Glances at label on the sofa.*) I'm pleased you've finally decided to take this sofa.

TONY. Have you remembered why you don't like it?

AUDREY. No and it's been driving me mad! That's why I'm glad it's going. Did I catch you groping my sister in it?

TONY. No that was in the larder at Putney one Christmas.

AUDREY. You were very drunk I remember. Well you'd have to be to fancy my sister.

TONY. Stella said she'd like the sofa.

AUDREY. When did she see it? You said she's never been here. That was another lie was it? (*TONY goes to reply.*) So she's been here in my absence and already decided what she wants?

TONY. I ...

AUDREY. You've always enjoyed making a fool of me. When did you bring her here to make her inventory? Bet she doesn't want anything I chose!

TONY. I did a drawing of the sofa. (*A beat.*) I also did a drawing of the corner cupboard and that occasional table.

AUDREY. Both of which I bought at the junk shop.

TONY. And she said she'd love to have them if you no longer wanted them.

AUDREY. (*Feeling foolish, SHE tidies the room.*) She's most welcome to them.

TONY. And when I told her we still had Lucy's old cot upstairs she said she'd quite like this too. You haven't any further use for it have you?

AUDREY. Not personally, no ... Tony... As you ... well know my period of usefulness as a woman has long since passed!

TONY. I was only asking if...?

AUDREY. I was keeping it for when Lucy had a baby.

TONY. Fine. I'll buy a new one. I'll take it back upstairs.

AUDREY. No, I'd like it used. Lucy is not going to have a baby just yet. I hope.

TONY. Right. Stella said to make sure it still worked before I brought it. I haven't quite got the hang of it yet.

AUDREY. You never did get the hang of it. You only once managed to put it up on your own. The night it collapsed with Mark in it. I'm sure it was that that made him wet his bed till he was twelve.

TONY. I knew I'd done something to him you could never forgive. I got this bit right ... this bit swings out ...

AUDREY. That's what you said twenty-two years ago. You've always been hopeless about this cot.

TONY. It's because it's wooden. My woodwork master gave me a thing about wood. I was two years making this table at school and every Friday he'd come round, look at it then hit me on the head with it.

AUDREY. Was that the teacher who said you'd end up on the scaffold?

TONY. No, that was the chaplain.

AUDREY. Well take that rod out for a start.

(HE props the cot up against the sofa and removes the rod.)

AUDREY. Then you get this side. (*SHE goes to the opposite side.*) ... which is the side that doesn't slide.

TONY. Slide! Not swing! Yes! It's all coming back!

AUDREY. There should be some screws in a bag somewhere ... (*SHE finds a little bag tied to the wire spring.*) Ah yes ... (*Opens the bag.*) Gone a bit rusty ...

TONY. This is the side that slides?

(*HE refers to his side of the cot. AUDREY, sorting out the screws does not look up. HE picks up the side panel. SHE looks up.*)

AUDREY. No, that is the side that doesn't. (*SHE goes back to the bag.*)

TONY. This is not the side that slides?

AUDREY. No. That side screws.

TONY. (*HE puts the panel down and examines his side of the cot.*)This is the side that screws? (*HE stares at it ... baffled.*)

AUDREY. Yes.

TONY. So it 's your side that slides?

AUDREY. No, ... Tony This is the side that screws. (*SHE collects a side panel.*)

TONY. Ah! You meant the *side*!

AUDREY. I said that. (*SHE connects up her side.*) Now pay attention, Tony. I've been showing you how to do this since Mark was born and he's now twenty-four and a bank manager in Kenya. This is the very last demonstration I'm going to give you.

TONY. Right. I'm all ears.

AUDREY. These screws go into these four holes this side ... comme ci ... comme ca ... comme ci ... comme ca ... Having secured this side ... (*SHE comes round to his side.*) I take this rod with the red mark on top ... which matches the red mark on the left hand side of the cot. I insert it through the top screw eye, the top and bottom hole of the side and into the lower screw eye. I then do the same on the right side.

TONY. What are these red marks?

AUDREY. They are the remains of my old nail varnish. I dabbed it on because the left rod doesn't like going into the right hand screw eye. I marked the left rod at the top and the right rod at the bottom. (*Looks at mark closely.*) Oh I say! Do you remember those ghastly shades of nail varnish we had years ago? ... You wouldn't perhaps ... Anyway ... the left rod has a red mark level with this mark here ... and the right rod has a red mark on the bottom here (*Points to red mark at lower end.*) ... which matches the red mark down here on the cot. So ... everything now in place, you press these two side catches ... lift up a few inches to clear and you can then lower the side. (*SHE does so.*) ... like this. You want to raise the side? You slide it up ... press the catches over these two bits and it rests ... presto!

TONY. Ah!

AUDREY. (*Picks up the mattress.*) You'll need to air this thoroughly, of course, but having done that ... you place it in ... and there! It's all ready for your nice new daughter.

TONY. Thank you.

AUDREY. So you can dismantle it now and take it. I don't want it hanging about here.

TONY. Could I just study it for a few more moments before I do so?

AUDREY. Don't take ages. (*SHE takes two bottles of champagne into the kitchen.*)

TONY. (*Stares at the cot.*) Left has top red mark, right has bottom red mark. That side screws, this side slides, press catches down ... lift up to clear ... then down ... release catches.

(*AUDREY returns with a cloth and some plates. TONY takes out his diary and begins to make notes.*)

TONY. I wish I'd known earlier you were getting married today!
AUDREY. Why? Did you want to buy me a wedding present? What sort of thing had you in mind?
TONY. I ... (*Suddenly defeated.*) ... oh hell no, what can I say to you now, but wish you luck? And I do Audrey. I wish you all the luck in the world.
AUDREY. Thank you Tony. Where is Brian? He's cutting it rather fine and Lucy's train will be arriving in five minutes.

(*TONY begins to dismantle the cot. HE exits with cot and returns for the mattress.*

AUDREY. I think she'd like it if I met her. (*Graciously to Tony.*) I don't suppose you'll be here when I get back, Tony, so I'll say cheerio now.
TONY. Right. Cheerio! All the best!
AUDREY. Thank you. (*SHE collects her car keys.*)
TONY. Off you go and meet Lucy. I'll just clear up these few remaining bits and pieces and then be off myself.
AUDREY. Okay. Bye. (*SHE leaves ... irritated.*)

(TONY looks around the room, finds something that interests him. CAR drives off. HE looks up and around the room, remembering ... Then the sound of modern MUSIC is heard and the sound gets louder.)

TONY. It can only mean one thing. My daughter approaches. *(Smiles.)*

(HE goes to the door and opens it. The MUSIC gets louder then LUCY appears in a 40's dress and a bright green streak in her hair. She is eighteen. SHE dances to the music in a casual, unconscious way.)

LUCY. Hi Dad.
TONY. Will you turn it down half a decibel?

(SHE turns down her cassette which hangs from a shoulder strap.)

TONY. You've made it in time for the wedding.
LUCY. Well I could do with a giggle. I've been on Coroners' inquests all this week and that's not a barrel of laughs. Where's Mum?
TONY. She went to meet you.
LUCY. I told her I'd make my own way from the station. She never listens to anything I say ... silly faggot!
TONY. How did you get here?
LUCY. Some red faced farmer gave me a lift. He stopped and said ... *(Her country accent.)* ... 'ello moi 'andsome ... oi be goin' down end of lane if you wanna lift me dear? Ooooh ahhhr ... *(SHE moos like a cow.)* ... So I

jumped in. (*Sees the food and the bottle of champagne.*)
Cor! Mum's pushing the boat out. Shall we have a drop to
get us in the party mood? Might put the colour back in
your cheeks. (*Hands bottle to Tony.*) You open it, Dad. I'll
get some ice. (*SHE goes into the kitchen. Enters with a
tray of ice cubes and two glasses.*). Where's the groom?
     TONY. (*HE catches hold of her cassette and turns it
off.*) He hasn't arrived yet. (*TONY opens the champagne.*)
     LUCY. You're allowed a little medicinal champagne
these days, aren't you?
     TONY. Definitely. (*HE pours out two glasses.*)
     LUCY. Well here's to 'em!
     TONY. Bless 'em all!

(*THEY drink.*)

     LUCY. I had no idea Mum was getting married till she
phoned me last night. I tried to phone you but I'd forgotten
the name of your hotel. When did you know?
     TONY. About twenty minutes ago.
     LUCY. I was amazed! She ... (*SHE goes quickly to
the conservatory window and looks out.*) ... she can't love
him can she? (*SHE returns.*) He's been hanging round for
years, but she's never taken him seriously. Just used him
to take her out. It's going to be very embarrassing for me
... having him as my step-father.
     TONY. You'll get used to it. There's no harm in him
...
     LUCY. But you can't love him ... no one could *love*
him!

TONY. Who knows about anybody? All we can do now is hope it works out for her. She's always said she finds him very relaxing.

LUCY. That's true. She's always dropping off when she's with him. It's that daft Stella's fault, of course ... getting her dates wrong and staggering up here and practically having the baby on your doorstep. That's who we've got to thank. That is what has triggered it all off. I bet my bottom dollar on that.

TONY. Not sure ... anyway, we can't blame Stella.

LUCY. But you would never have brought her along for the ride if you'd known she was due last week!

TONY. No, but then I should have checked. I know what she's like. She never has known what day it is.

LUCY. I'm very disappointed Dad.

TONY. (*Shrugs.*) It's probably all for the best. If I had found the right moment to tell Mum I doubt if it would have changed things.

LUCY. I'm still cross though.

TONY. Yes you've worked quite hard on your little scheme haven't you? I'm sorry you feel let down but I didn't expect much to come of it ... even if I had managed to tell her.

LUCY. You didn't even find *one* moment when you might have?

TONY. No. Don't go on at me.

LUCY. I won't.

TONY. I tried ... that's all I can say.

LUCY. I'm sure you did Dad.

TONY. Had I succeeded it might have led somewhere. We might have found out if there was a way of picking up the bits. Probably not. Anyway, I'm sure it was only a phase I was going through. (*Smiles.*) I'll get over it!

LUCY. It's my mistake. I gave you a bum steer in the first place.

TONY. I must admit I never *saw* any sign of this softening you told me about. I couldn't reach her ... no how. Couldn't touch her at all. I don't think anyone can now. (*Looks at his watch.*) I'd better go. It's visiting time.

LUCY. You're having a drink with us afterwards? Just to wish Mum good luck?

TONY. I haven't been asked.

(*A CAR is heard arriving as he picks up the mattress. As HE opens the door AUDREY enters and sees Lucy.*)

AUDREY Oh! You're here
TONY. I'm just going.
AUDREY. No, Lucy! Did you get a taxi from ...

(*LUCY turns to her and SHE sees the green side of Lucy's hair.*)

AUDREY. My God! Darling! You haven't come down in the train like that!

LUCY. Yes but I can easily go back on it if you want me to.

TONY. (*Diplomatically.*) Well I'll leave you to it. (*HE goes to exit.*)

LUCY. You haven't invited Dad to wish you good luck after your wedding.

AUDREY. (*Hesitates for a moment.*) Only because I know he wouldn't want to come.

LUCY. Ask him.

TONY. No, please. I 'm going now.

AUDREY. You'd be most welcome Tony to drop in for a glass of something with Brian and myself around four. You know that. I don't have to tell you.

TONY. Thank you. I'd be delighted.

AUDREY. (*Thin smile.*) Good!

(HE exits.)

AUDREY. I just thought it would be nicer just to keep it family.

LUCY. Dad is.

AUDREY. He's ex-family.

LUCY. He's not my ex-father. How's Brian. Getting twitchy? Is he looking forward to becoming my step-father?

AUDREY. Lucy, could you, for once, stop making fun of Brian? Last week when you came to tea you never stopped laughing at him.

LUCY. Only because I'd never seen anyone hoover a lawn before.

AUDREY. I don't make fun of your friends.

LUCY. Then why did you say that Rodney's eyes reminded you of two currants in a rock cake?

AUDREY. It's your hair I wish to discuss, Lucy. Don't change the subject. What are we going to do about it? Could you put it up in a style where the green is slightly less obtrusive?

LUCY. No.

AUDREY. No, I didn't think you could. Well, I haven't time to argue, I'm late already so I'd be very grateful if you could wash the salad things for me.

LUCY. Okay. (*SHE collects a lettuce and some spring onions from the box.*)

AUDREY. Then when Brian and I pop off you can change.

LUCY. Change what?

AUDREY. Your dress, of course. You said you'd bought a lovely dress for my wedding.

LUCY. This is it.

AUDREY. Darling, I'm not in the mood for any more leg pulling. I'm getting one of my hot flushes as it is. Where's your bag? You can get changed in your old room. There's that nice big mirror in there.

LUCY. I came just like this. No bag.

(Pause.)

AUDREY. Lucy, I asked you down here for a specific purpose, to be here when Brian and I returned from the Registry Office so that you would give me the infinite and lasting joy of proposing my future happiness!

LUCY. I can do that in this dress. Look! (*SHE raises her glass.*) It gives me great pleasure to ...

AUDREY. Lucy! You can't wear that dress at my wedding!

LUCY. Okay ... I'll take it off. I'll propose your future happiness in my bra and pants!

AUDREY. Fortunately, I have my little pink dress upstairs and you can borrow that, so all is not lost. (*SHE smiles with maternal satisfaction.*)

LUCY. I'm not wearing one of my mother's dresses.
AUDREY. But you love wearing old ladies' clothes!
LUCY. But you're not old enough.
AUDREY. That's the nicest thing you've ever said to me. No, I'm sorry darling ... but I really can't have you proposing my happiness looking exactly like that old snap of my Auntie Lottie on D. Day.
LUCY. (*Delighted.*) Really? That's the nicest thing you've ever said to *me*! Or are you just saying that?
AUDREY. (*Cross but more than a suggestion of desperate tears lurking.*) Lucy ... don't you even care a *little* about my feelings? Can't you love me just for a day? How can you turn up here wearing something you've just grabbed hold of in a Boy Scouts jumble sale? (*SHE fumbles in her bag for her hanky.*) I'm sorry ... but it really upsets me to have my only daughter dressed like a bag lady on my wedding day. Looking as if she's just stepped out of a second hand shop!

(LUCY turns on her cassette loud and exits the front door ... slamming it. Silence. Door bell. AUDREY answers it. LUCY enters.)

LUCY. My friend Sally phoned up and said the local Oxfam shop had just had a fabulous new load of gear delivered. Next day we queued for an hour before they opened. There were half a dozen girls in front of us. I saw this dress inside ... that's it I said. Perfect for Mum's wedding ... padded shoulders ... the big lapels ... the genuine forties length ... everything you could want ... The doors opened and we all charged in. One of the other girls got it first. I could have died! Then I saw this white chiffon blouse with the droopy bows and the genuine period buttons ... just like the one Ingrid Bergman wore in "Casablanca." I grabbed it. This girl went green with envy. I'll swop I said. Right she said. So I got it. I didn't just grab it at a jumble sale. I didn't just *happen* to find these genuine 1942 sandals with the genuine utility mark and the genuine cuban heels and ankle straps. I've had them waiting for months ... for the right dress ... the special occasion. (*Her tears well up.*) I've really thought about your wedding day, Mum. You're not fair to say I don't care. That I don't bother with you ... I only bother with Dad. Not true. I spent a long time making myself look nice for you. Maybe it's not your style but I have tried. That's it with you ... you never know when people are trying to please you.

LUCY. Oh darling ... please ... (*AUDREY blows her nose*)

LUCY. You always say I only love Dad. (*LUCY takes Audrey's hanky and blows her nose on it.*)

AUDREY. Oh Lucy, darling! Please don't cry on my wedding day. (*Takes her hanky back.*)

LUCY. You're so hard and unforgiving. There's nothing soft in you any more. Dad's quite right when he says no one can touch you now. (*SHE goes up the stairs.*)

(*AUDREY stares for a moment then looks at her watch. SHE goes out to the conservatory. AUDREY returns to the room and gets some groceries from the box and takes them into the kitchen.*
LUCY comes down the stairs dressed in a pink linen dress and with her hair arranged to cover most of the green streak. AUDREY comes out.)

AUDREY. Very nice. Thank you. Will you sit there and talk to me for a moment?

(*LUCY sits in an easy chair. AUDREY sits on the sofa.*)

AUDREY. What did you mean ... Dad can't touch me any more?

LUCY. Oh Mum ... you don't really care what he says do you?

AUDREY. No. Not at all but please tell me.

LUCY. (*Hesitates.*) He told me in confidence.

AUDREY. You've always got on better with him, of course. You started to take his side when you were six!

LUCY. (*Kindly.*) Mum ... you and I can't live together but I do love you. Don't confuse the two.

AUDREY. I find it hard to find the dividing line sometimes.

LUCY. I think Dad has the same difficulty with Mark.

AUDREY. At least one of my children likes living with me.

LUCY. Well, that's fair isn't it? One each?

AUDREY. But you tell Dad things I tell you in confidence. Is that fair?

LUCY. No ... it's just how it's worked out. And you have got a big mouth, Mum. Let's face it. You can't keep anything to yourself. You'd be bound to tell him one day. If you've got the ammunition you've got to use it. You've never been able to resist scoring and having alienated one parent, I've no ambition to try for the double.

AUDREY. If I'm hard, I'm only what ...

LUCY. ... "your father has made me." Yes ... he agrees with that now. He knows he's hurt you too much. He knows now that you and he are beyond repair.

AUDREY. Knows now!? (*Laughs.*) He decided that years ago. That's a good one! He knows *now!* (*SHE gives a derisive snort.*)

LUCY. (*Suddenly but casually.*) Stella's baby is not his. (*LUCY does not look at Audrey.*)

(*AUDREY slowly turns and looks at her. Their eyes meet for a moment.*)

LUCY. Oh God! (*SHE rises and kneels by the table and puts her hand over her eyes. Pause. SHE rises.*) I just had to say a quick prayer.

AUDREY. For what?

LUCY. That it doesn't get back to him. I'll kill you if it does, Mum. I mean it. I'll throttle you. From behind. I've worked it all out already.

AUDREY. He is not the father?

LUCY. Steve is. (*SHE kneels again and prays.*)

AUDREY. Steve is Juliet's father? (*Pause.*) Will you please stand up and pay attention, Lucy? (*LUCY rises.*) The young man who does exercises in your living room?

LUCY. Yes.

AUDREY. Your father is not Juliet's father?

LUCY. No.

AUDREY. I've *never* had such a flush as this! (*SHE lies out delicately on the sofa with her hand over her eyes. Pause.*) Well? Don't stop now.

LUCY. Dad has never told you the whole truth about why he left home.

AUDREY. He left me because he was bored with me. Don't deny it at this late stage ... please!

LUCY. I'm not. You were making him unhappy but he had another reason for going. That was the doctor telling him that unless he packed up the booze he'd be dead inside a year.

AUDREY. (*Half rising.*) Doctor? What doctor? Our Dr. McNab?

LUCY. Yes.

AUDREY. I never knew. Why wasn't I told?

LUCY. Dad didn't want to tell you because he didn't want your sympathy. You weren't getting on with each other and he thought that his cirrhosis of the liver would only cloud the issue. He decided that he had to live on his own to sort his boozing out *and* your life together.

AUDREY. Please continue.

LUCY. Well when Dad went to live in Hackney, Stella lived with Steve in the next room. Three months later Steve left and Stella went next door to Dad and cried on his shoulder. Steve came back a fortnight later and she went back. Then he left and Stella went next door to Dad. Then Steve came home again ...

AUDREY. (*Faintly.*) I think I could manage a very tiny glass of champagne please Lucy. (*SHE sits up slowly.*) I suddenly feel in need of a lift.

(*LUCY pours her out a glass.*)

AUDREY. Your father always said that he and Stella *lived* together.

LUCY. Oh yes ... they might have done something now and then ... but they never fancied each other much.

She was very good at doing his laundry and that appealed to Dad very much.

AUDREY. I have never heard Steve's name mentioned before last Monday and then your father only referred to him as a temporary lodger.

LUCY. Why should he tell you?

AUDREY. No. That's right.

LUCY. You did laugh at his paintings ...

AUDREY. But I never knew ... I was never told ... I laughed at that time in order to shock him into the realisation that he was not a painter but a photographer ...

LUCY. And you were right but shouldn't have laughed. The third time Steve left to go and live in Borth-y-Llangyderch, he was gone for five months. Stella and Dad settled down to a nice quiet life together. It wasn't a great love affair for either of them, but Dad found it cosy. One day he came back from a fish finger commercial in Alaska and there was a note saying she'd gone to live with Steve forever. Three months later she came back two months pregnant ... September last year. She asked Dad to fix up an abortion ... Dad was shocked, of course. Oh yes. We all know, under that bohemian, rakish exterior of his, there beats a very moral Baptist heart. So ... he tears off to Borth-y-Llangyderch and tells Steve he must marry Stella or he'll do him up. Steve said no. Dad went to punch him on the nose but Steve ducked and Dad missed. Steve then went to punch Dad in the eye and didn't. Dad comes back, offers to marry Stella to ... I now quote Dad's words ... to give the baby a name. Well, it occurred to the ever devious Stella that it might just do the trick with Steve if she had his baby, so she said yes. So Dad married her—the following week. A month later Stella proved to be right because Steve turns up and has been living with us, on and off, ever since. And now that Steve has a baby daughter he wants to move into this flat with Stella and the baby.

AUDREY. What flat?

LUCY. The flat Dad has got for them. Stella is very pleased about the way it's all worked out.

AUDREY. That is why your father suddenly decided to take some of the furniture?

LUCY. That was Stella's idea. Dad was going to buy them new stuff. Well ... that's what he said to me on the phone last night. Then you phoned and said you were getting married today.

AUDREY. And the future?

LUCY. Dad is going to arrange for Stella to divorce him on the grounds of complete breakdown of marriage.

AUDREY. Why are you telling me all this?

LUCY. Because Dad wanted to tell you on Monday but lost his bottle ... I'm doing it for him.

AUDREY. Why did he want to tell me?

LUCY. Because he's been very worried about it for months. Whether he'd done the right thing. He wanted reassurance.

AUDREY. Which you no doubt gave him?

LUCY. But my values don't mean much to him. He only respects the views of people who are middle-aged, middle class and preferably have a BMW. He made up his mind to speak to you after I had tea with you. I went home and said I think you could talk to Mum now. There was a softness ... a ... a ... I don't know ... vulnerability perhaps ... there was something about you I hadn't seen before.

AUDREY. Your father has not once hinted that he wanted some help. All I got was a phone call from him saying he'd like some of the furniture before we sold the cottage and would like to sort it out with me.

LUCY. Yes, I invented the furniture as an excuse, so that if Dad found he couldn't tell you, he could get out without showing his hand—without you knowing he had need of you.

AUDREY. But he is so happy! He was so thrilled about Juliet!

LUCY. Why not? Juliet will always be a part of him. He's told Stella that he hopes Juliet will always look upon him as her funny old Uncle. But he's on his own, Mum, so you've no cause to think that life has given him a better deal than it's given you. You're better off in fact. He doesn't have anyone who wants to marry him.

AUDREY. (*Rises and collects her dress and hat.*) You had absolutely no right to tell me this.

LUCY. I know.

(SHE goes to kneel but AUDREY stops her.)

AUDREY. It's too late to pray now! I'm marrying Brian in forty minutes! Forty minutes and I haven't even changed or got my face on! You can't tell me this now, Lucy! I won't have it. I shall forget everything you've said!

LUCY. Please do.

AUDREY. Brian adores me and I am a very lucky woman!

LUCY. You are! Did you know that a divorced woman over forty has less chance of getting remarried than a man of eighty?

AUDREY. Because a woman of my age can't give a man a new family. I've only myself to offer ... complete with menopausal hot flushes, but Brian is over the moon to have me just as I am. He's over the moon!

LUCY. I'm sure he is, Mum. You must marry him. You may not get a second chance.

AUDREY. Exactly! As it is, it's the only offer I've had since I've been on my own.

LUCY. Take it ! Take it, Mum.

AUDREY. I will! I will!

LUCY. You must! You must!

AUDREY. I want to know nothing more about your father's matrimonial arrangements. I just want to concentrate on my own!

LUCY. You've got to!

AUDREY. And all I want now is for you to wash the lettuce and be here when we come back looking like my nice, pretty daughter and for you to wish us both health, wealth and happiness for our future life together.

LUCY. I will! I will! Promise you, Mum! I'll do the lettuce now! (*LUCY goes into the kitchen.*)

(*AUDREY goes up the stairs.*
MUSIC comes loud from the kitchen.
LIGHTS fade
LIGHTS come up.
LUCY is arranging the food.
TONY is in the conservatory looking out at the garden. HE
    glances at his watch, comes in and dials the phone.)

LUCY. Is it all right?

TONY. Very nice. Mum'll be pleased. (*Into phone.*) The Registry Office for marriages please.

LUCY. Would you like a glass of champagne Dad? This bottle is going a bit flat. You're allowed the odd glass aren't you?

TONY. Certainly.

(LUCY pours out two glasses.)

TONY. *(Into phone.)* Good afternoon. Some friends of mine are getting married at your office this afternoon. Could you tell me if the ceremony has been performed yet? Audrey Holland and Brian Chibnall. Thank you. *(LUCY hands him a glass.)* Hello? I see. Thank you very much. Goodbye. *(HE hangs up. A beat.)* Audrey Louisa Holland and Brian Cecil Arthur Chibnall were married half an hour ago.

LUCY. So I've got a bonny bouncing new step-father?

TONY. You have. Is your glass charged my daughter?

LUCY. Yes.

TONY. Then I'd like to propose a toast to the health, wealth and happiness of the bride and groom. The bride and groom!

LUCY. The bride and groom !

(THEY both drink.)

TONY. Now before I go ...

LUCY. Go? You said you were going to stay to wish them well?

TONY. I just have. Has your cassette got one of those built in mics? *(HE examines it.)*

LUCY. Yes.

TONY. Good. I shall leave them a parting message.

LUCY. I haven't got a spare tape.

TONY. I shall put my message on top of Bob Dylan or whoever it is. He won't like it but it's the best we can do.

LUCY. He'll never sound the same again.

TONY. I'll buy you a new one. (*HE picks up the cassette and presses the controls. We hear a snatch of Bob Dylan singing "Changing of the Guard."*)

LUCY. You press that other knob for record.

(*HE does so. Silence*)

TONY. (*Into mic.*) Dear Audrey and dear Brian ...

(*A CAR is heard arriving.*)

TONY. Ah! The happy bride and groom have arrived ... the bride radiant in her azure blue with matching accessories. I'll go to the potting shed. (*TONY exits through conservatory door carrying his glass of champagne and the cassette.*)

(*LUCY opens the front door. AUDREY enters.*)

LUCY. Shouldn't Brian carry you in?

AUDREY. Where's your father? His van is blocking up the drive again and Brian can't park his car.

LUCY. In the potting shed. Congratulations Mum. (*SHE kisses Audrey.*)

AUDREY. Thank you my darling.

LUCY. The champagne and everything is all ready.

AUDREY. You've done it very nicely dear ... now would you be an absolute angel and catch the next train back to London?

LUCY. But we haven't had the wedding breakfast!

AUDREY. The wedding breakfast is off dear!

LUCY. Off? But you've just got married!

AUDREY. Yes but the moment we left the town hall we both realised it was a mistake. And it was a very lovely ceremony ... Lovely. I enjoyed it immensely. But the moment we were married we both realised it would spoil our friendship ... (*Pause.*) Well it does doesn't it? Your generation knows that so much better than mine. So we went and had a nice cup of tea in the Cathedral tea rooms and I said I had only done it to please him ... And Brian said he had only done it to please me. Which is the test of true friendship. It's not often one puts ones friends to the test ... But we tested each other today ... And we're both delighted to find out that neither of us were lacking.

LUCY. You're not going to blame me are you Mum?

AUDREY. Blame you for what Lucy?

LUCY. (*Nervously.*) I don't know. Perhaps it was something I said. You've always said I was a mixer.

AUDREY. Darling! When did I ever say such a cruel thing?

LUCY. You first said it to me when I was twelve.

AUDREY. You've always had an implacable memory, of course. Darling, I don't blame you for anything. I'm very grateful to you, in fact, for making me realise that your dreadful father ... that devious ... mixed up ... appalling father of yours came here on Monday ... not to sort out this furniture ... but because he wanted to see if I still cared for him. Had you told me a little earlier the true facts of his life, I might have been more receptive to his needs ... I might have twigged what was behind his visit. But you didn't tell me and I was in total ignorance. It never occurred to me for a moment that your father was as lonely as myself. I didn't know any of these things but now I see that last Monday ... under your father's vitriolic tongue ... he was trying to say he still cared for me. He was trying to ... to ... open the gates. He was sort of asking me if I was still available.

LUCY. But you've just got married to Brian.

AUDREY. Technically yes, but I'm keeping myself available *emotionally*. It is true that I'm not free to marry now ... But then neither is your father. Your mother has only done what your father did. So that we are now both in the same boat. That is all that has happened, Lucy ... I'm now in the same boat as your father.

LUCY. I see.

AUDREY. Brian is waiting to drive you to the station or to London if you like. I don't want to chuck you out, Lucy. (*Pause.*) Your father and I have got a lot of rough ground to travel over before we can speak to each other like normal, civilised people but I think we'll make it in time. Thank you for giving us a new beginning, darling. (*SHE gives Lucy a hurried embrace.*) Please go now.

(*LUCY goes to the door. We hear a CAR start up.*)

LUCY. I'll ring you, Mum.
AUDREY. Yes please.

(*TONY enters with cassette.
LUCY exits.*

*AUDREY goes up to the window and waves them good-
bye. SHE then goes briskly to the conservatory, opens
the door and calls out. SHE returns and eats a piece of
pork pie then pours two glasses of champagne.)*

TONY. Congratulations !

AUDREY. Thank you.

TONY. Where's the happy groom?

AUDREY. He's just taken Lucy to the station.

TONY. Oh! I could have given her a lift back. I'm
picking Stella up at the hospital in five minutes.

AUDREY. You're not staying for my wedding
breakfast?

TONY. Is there a French word called de trop?

AUDREY. Two words—meaning superfluous.

TONY. That's me. I'm Mr. De Trop at this moment.
You didn't want me here. I didn't want to come. It was just
another of Lucy's mad ideas and we both wanted to oblige
her. Well ... I didn't really think you'd go through with it
but you have, which just proves how right you were.

AUDREY. About what?

TONY. About me not understanding you.

AUDREY. Tony I know you can't stand the sight of
me and I don't want to discuss the past any more ...

TONY. Nor me ... you and I can't speak more than two
sentences to each other before we're at each other's throats.

AUDREY. That's right.

TONY. That is why I've left you a little message ...
with my love, Audrey. (*Hands her the cassette recorder.*)
You'll probably shriek with laughter at it. It will probably
inspire you to make a lot of derisive comments, but at
least I won't know. This is what I want to say to you,

Audrey ... play it or throw it in the dustbin. (*Goes up to the door*.) I'm off now.

AUDREY. All right Tony ... I do see ... you must be so very upset, but could I just say ...?

TONY. Send me a tape. I'll phone you. Let's have supper one day. Don't let it be another ten months!

AUDREY. I won't.

TONY. I'll always love you, Audrey ... in my way.

AUDREY. I'll always love you, Tony ... in my way.

(*HE waves. Goes ...*
SHE stands at the door.
The VAN is heard to start ... Crashing of gears. It drives off ...
SHE quietly closes the door. SHE brings the cassette down to the table ... SHE pours herself a glass of champagne and sits with it ... SHE examines the controls. Takes out her glasses and puts them on and examines the controls.)

AUDREY. Stop. Eject. Pause. Play. Cut. Review. Record. Ah yes! (*SHE deliberates for a moment, then presses a button. Bob Dylan singing ... A click.*)

TONY'S VOICE. One two three four five ... testing testing ...

AUDREY. Oh Tony ... you are so lovely!

(*The sounds of TONY clearing his throat. SHE sips her champagne and makes gurgling tender sounds throughout.*)

TONY'S VOICE. Dear Audrey, Dear Brian ... just a little message wishing you both good luck from the ex. I'm recording this because I don't have the nerve to stand up with a glass of champagne in my hand and tell you face to face. But I am toasting you, Audrey and Brian. My heart and thoughts are with you even if I'm not here in person. You'll just have to imagine me here with the glass of champagne. This has some advantages of course, because if you don't want me here any more you can just switch me off. You just press the button marked eject and I'm gone. Perhaps you've already done that but if not I'd just like to say ... thanks for our twenty marvellous years Audrey ... Of course some of them were a bit rough ... and I gave you many unhappy moments, but we had some good times too and that's what makes the time marvellous ... the ups and downs ... we both took the rough with the smooth and I'd do it again Audrey ... I would. I'd do it all over again. You're a smashing bird ... did you know that? No ... well why should you? I never told you. But you are ... a smashing bird.

AUDREY. Oh Tony ... (*The tears begin as SHE pours herself a second glass of champagne.*)

TONY'S VOICE. You kept me going so beautifully ... you stuck to *your* guns all right ... stuck to what you said those aeons of time ago in St. Mark's Church, Clapham ... when your dad had to sell his insurance policy to pay for the reception ... My God, *you* stuck to what you said in front of those two hundred and fifty assorted friends and relatives ... You cherished me all right ... comforted me ... honoured me ... sickness and in health ... you gave me two lovely babies ... you have been the most marvellous bloody wife to me, Audrey ... my love ... and I never knew it. I never knew it, my old darling

AUDREY. Oh Tony ... Oh Tony ... (*SHE pours herself more champagne ...*)

TONY'S VOICE. You took all my lies ... all my cheats ... all my deceptions ... you took the five card trick from me ... and still stayed smiling ... still stayed loving me. Through all the years my heart ... you were constant ... never faltered. But I? Do you know what I am, Audrey? I've finally realised just what I am. Instant shit.

AUDREY. Oh no darling! You mustn't say such things about yourself.

TONY'S VOICE. You just need to put a spoonful of me in a cup and add hot water and there you have me ... instant shit! I invented my sexual hang ups because I stopped fancying you. I always lied ... always denied it. I couldn't face you with it. Couldn't tell you I'd stopped fancying you my darling ... that I was incapable of responding to the wonderful devotion you gave me over twenty years. Only now ... when it is too late do I realise just what I had when you were my wife. It's only now ... I appreciate you. I will never get another chance for such happiness. I know that. I know it's too late now for both of us.

AUDREY. It isn't my darling ... It isn't! Thank God!

TONY'S VOICE. As for you, Brian ... all I can say to you is that if Audrey is one quarter the wife to you that she was to me you'll be a very happy man. And you will be, I know that. You will both be very happy together because you are a much better bloke than me, Brian. You know about love. I see the way you look at Audrey and I know you know. And there is only love isn't there? To be loved

... and be among those you love. Do make up for me a bit, Brian ... my lovely Audrey deserves it ... after twenty-one years with me.

AUDREY. Oh Tony! (*Tears.*)

TONY'S VOICE. I shall always miss you, Audrey. I came back to see you my darling ... because I had some lunatic idea that maybe we might start again.

AUDREY. Oh my dear darling ... (*Kisses the recorder.*)

TONY'S VOICE. But I soon realised that I came back simply because I was at a low ebb ... it was a momentary weakness ...

AUDREY. Oh darling ... please ... I can't bear it. (*SHE pours some more champagne and sniffs back her tears.*)

TONY'S VOICE. But I'm totally over that now.

(*SHE stops, blinks, alert.*)

TONY'S VOICE. ... completely and utterly. I'm sorry if I have embarrassed you or Brian by coming back into your lives. Well ... I'll sign off now and to close I just want to say that if Stella and I are only half as happy as I know you two will be, it'll be far more than I deserve. Stella and I haven't been good so far—for many reasons. One of them was I never thought I was the father of her child ... anyway, it turns out that I am and she loves me so everything is marvellous. It's suddenly got better today ... suddenly got miraculously better and I know you will both be pleased now that you two are so happy ... you'll both be pleased that at long last I've found a woman that I think I can love as she loves me. I never did it with you, Audrey. Anyway, it may not be too late for, me to be happy, even now when I'm well past half time. So ... here in the potting shed I raise my glass to you both ... Audrey and Brian and all the luck in the world.

(Silence and then a SCUFFLING, KNOCKING sound of Tony fiddling with the controls. A CLICK then Bob Dylan singing "True Love." SHE stares at the recorder for some moments then picks it up and tries to read the controls. Holds it out at arm's length. Still can't read it. Finds her glasses and puts them on and switches off the machine. Silence. SHE stares for a moment in a blank, bewildered way like someone lost. SHE then straightens the cushions on the sofa. That finished SHE looks round for something else to do. SHE collects some crockery and a plate of food and takes them out to the kitchen.
After a moment we hear FOOTSTEPS approaching over the shingle path. Front door opens and TONY enters. HE holds a marriage licence which has handwriting on the reverse. As HE looks round, AUDREY enters, head down and carrying a tray and wearing an apron. SHE does not see him standing there as SHE puts the glasses and the champagne on the tray. SHE works busily and does not seem distressed so that her sudden sob surprises us.)

AUDREY. Oh God. (*Stacks plates.*) I don't want to love that bastard. (*Wipes a plate with her tea towel.*) I don't! (*Empties wine glasses into ice bucket.*) I don't. You're not fair. It's not fair of you to make me like this ... incapable of loving another man. Please get that shit-house out of my life. Please stop me loving him! (*SHE takes her piled up tray to the kitchen.*)

TONY. I was driving to Salisbury ... (*SHE stops by the door but does not turn round.*) to pick Stella up from the hospital when I saw this piece of paper wedged into my ashtray. It's your marriage certificate. On the back of it Brian has written me a little note *(SHE rests her tray on the sideboard but still holds it.)* "Dear Tony, The only thing of value about this bit of paper is that it provides me with something to write on. I married Audrey to bring you back together. She married me because she loves you so much. If you can't understand that immediately don't bother to work it out. Yours, Brian."

TONY. *(HE comes down and tosses the note onto the tray then takes the champagne and two glasses from it.)* What a cow I thought! What a rotten cow. She's actually married harmless, old Brian ... just to get even with me. Made him marry her! Forced dear old, weak as piss Brian to marry her just in order to make me cross! *(HE hands her a glass of champagne.)* I'll show the cow I thought! *(Sips his drink and goes out to the conservatory and looks out down the garden.)* I am not the father of Stella's baby, of course.

AUDREY. I see.

TONY. Were you very upset when you played the tape and heard me say I was?

AUDREY. Very.

TONY. Oh good ... it was worth coming back then!

AUDREY. What a swine you are! No, really Tony, I never would have believed that I was capable of hating someone as much as I hate you! I'm really ashamed of the enmity I bear towards you! It makes me sick inside! I hate every bit of you, Tony. There's no part of you that I do not absolutely and totally loathe!

(Long pause.)

TONY. (*Calmly sips his champagne.*) So I suppose a fuck is out of the question?

(*SHE does not react just stares at him balefully as HE comes in and lies on the sofa.*)

TONY. Yes ... well ... you've only been married ... (*Glances at watch.*) seventy-five minutes so I suppose it is a bit early for you to take a lover. What do you think, Mrs. Chibnall? Are you in the mood to have a lover now that you're a respectable married woman? If so ... do pencil me in. I would like to be on your short list.

(*Pause.*)

AUDREY. No really Tony ... sometimes I actually astonish myself when I realise how much I dislike you. (*SHE takes off her dingle dangle earrings.*) I tell you this ... and I'm speaking right from my heart ... I rue the day I met you! (*Takes off her shoes and goes to the windows and draws the curtains.*) If I had only known that knowing you would lead to twenty-six years of purgatory ... (*SHE sits on the sofa by his knees.*) I would have run a mile! No really Tony ... I'll never forgive you ... for ruining my life! Are you listening? Don't go to sleep! I've only got one life and you've totally ruined it! No, I tell you Tony. I rue the day you walked into my life. Rue the day!

CURTAIN

PROPERTY PLOT

ACT I

On stage:

Corner cupboard
Telephone w/directory
Sofa
Dining table with four chairs
Occasional table
Book shelves w/books and telephone answering machine
Easy chair
Tie on and stick on labels
Bag with green, red and black felt pens
Sideboard w/Audrey's handbag
Glasses and bottle of sherry

Kitchen section:

Two bags of groceries
Basic kitchen utensils
Electric percolator with coffee
Box of tissues
Vacuum cleaner
Plastic bucket w/champagne (hidden)
Tray set with two mugs for coffee including plate of home-
    made shortcake

Conservatory section:

Dried up plants in pots on greenhouse staging
Live vine w/leaves and root going outside

Offstage:

Trowel
Pot of peonies in bud
Gardening gloves
Overnight bag

ACT II

On stage:

Furniture with written labels
Car keys

Kitchen section:

Brush
Tea cloth
Plates
Ice cubes in fridge
Plastic bucket as ice bucket

Offstage:

Sections of baby's cot with hinged sides, wire base and
    mattress wrapped in old newspaper
Parcels (Audrey) including dress and hat in bag
Groceries including port pie
Baby's clothes in bag
Walkman cassette
Diary (Tony)
Hanky (Audrey)
Watch (Tony)
Marriage license (Tony)
Tray and apron (Audrey)
Earrings (Audrey)

www.ingramcontent.com/pod-product-compliance
Lightning Source LLC
Chambersburg PA
CBHW070352120726
47909CB00008B/2816